Greenwillow
Read-alone

MENJ !

by NICKI WEISS

GREENWILLOW BOOKS
New York

Printed in U.S.A.   First Edition   10 9 8 7 6 5 4 3 2 1

Library of Congress Cataloging in Publication Data
Weiss, Nicki.   Menj!   (Greenwillow read-alone books)
Summary: During one day Francine argues with
her sister, makes a collection with the neighbor
boy, bakes chocolate chipless cookies, and
talks with her imaginary friend.
[. Frogs–Fiction]   I. Title.
PZ7.W448145Me   [Fic]   80-15955
ISBN 0-688-80306-7   ISBN 0-688-84306-9 (lib. bdg.)

FOR MY MOTHER

CONTENTS

MENJ!

One morning Francine woke up
and said "Good morning"
to her big sister Norma.

"MENJ!" said Norma.

"What did you say?"

Francine asked.

"I said MENJ!"

Francine thought for a minute.

"What does that mean?"

"You'll never know.

MENJ, MENJ, MENJ!"

Norma said.

And with that

she put on her slippers

and went down

to the kitchen.

At the breakfast table
Francine stuck out her tongue
at Norma.

"I don't care
about your dumb old word,"
she said.

But when Francine poured
some cereal into her bowl,
Norma said, "MENJ!"

And when she reached for the milk,
Norma said, "MENJ!"

And when she opened her mouth
for a spoonful of cornflakes,
Norma said, "MENJ!"

"Norma," Francine said,

"tell me what it means."

"Why should I?" asked Norma.

Francine said,

"I'll give you a crayon."

"I want all of them," said Norma.

She took the whole box.

First she scribbled
with the green crayon
until it was flat.
Then she scribbled
with the red crayon
until there wasn't
anything left.
Then she scribbled
with the gold crayon
until it broke.

Then she looked up
at Francine
and said, "MENJ!"

"Oh, MENJ yourself,

you big MENJ!"

Francine said.

She marched out of the kitchen.

A COLLECTION

After breakfast,

there was a knock

on the back door.

"Francine," Mrs. Treefrog called,

"Henry is here to play with you."

"Yuk," said Norma.

"You play with boys."

"What should we play today,
Francine?" Henry asked.

"How about making
a collection!" Francine said.

"We can look
in your backyard."

"Okay," said Henry,

"but we can't make noise.

My great-grandpa is sleeping

on the back porch.

He gets mad

if you wake him up."

"Shhh," said Francine.

Francine walked around the garden.

She picked up a gray stone.

She picked some weeds.

Then she found a caterpillar.

"Wow!" she said.

Henry bent down

to look at the ground.

He found a rusty screw.

And some more weeds.

He picked up

some broken branches

and some black ants

from the porch step.

"This is swell!" Henry said.

"Look at all these great things."

"Wait." Francine pulled up

a handful of grass.

"There," she said.

"What a terrific collection,"
said Henry.
"And it's so pretty!"
Francine said.
"Shhh, you'll wake up
my great-grandpa,"
Henry said.
"Let's go to your house
and give it to your mother."

Mrs. Treefrog looked out

the back door.

"My, my," she said.

"That's a very nice collection.

But why don't you

leave it outside?"

"Maybe we should see
if your mother will like it,"
Francine said.

"Okay," Henry said,
"but we must be very quiet
when we walk on the porch."

"Shhh," said Francine.

"Shhh," said Henry.

"Oh, dear," Henry's mother said.
"So interesting.
But perhaps it would be better
if you left that outside.
And don't wake Great-grandpa."

"Gee," Henry said.

"I don't think they liked it."

"Shhh," Francine said

as they tiptoed

on the porch.

Just then Great-grandpa

sat up in his chair.

"What's all the racket?

Who woke me up?

What have you two got there?"

"For me?" Great-grandpa asked.
"Why, thank you!"

CHOCOLATE CHIP COOKIES

In the late afternoon,
Mrs. Treefrog said,
"I'm going to bake
chocolate chip cookies.
You girls can help me."

Norma loved to bake.

"Sure, Mom," she said.

Francine loved chocolate chips.

She said, "Oh, boy!"

Mrs. Treefrog said,
"I'll get the eggs."
Norma said,
"I'll measure the flour
and the sugar."
"I'll count
the chocolate chips,"
said Francine.
"You just want
to eat them,"
said Norma.

Mrs. Treefrog poured everything
into a big bowl.
They took turns mixing.

"Stop picking out the chips,"
Norma said.

"Here's a cookie sheet
for each of you,"
their mother said.
"You can make
your own cookies."

The kitchen began to smell good.

When the cookies were done,

Mrs. Treefrog took them

out of the oven.

"I like chocolate chip cookies best
when they're hot," Norma said.
She took one off her cookie sheet.

Francine ate a cookie
from her cookie sheet.

"I like chocolate chip cookies best
when there are chocolate chips
in them," she said.

BORIS

That night, Mrs. Treefrog
tucked her girls into bed.
"Good night, dear,"
she said to Norma.
She gave her a kiss.
"And a kiss for you, too,"
she said to Francine.

When the room was all dark,

Francine reached

under her bed.

She pulled out

her invisible telephone.

And she dialed

her invisible friend Boris.

"Hi, Boris, I'm glad

you are home,"

she whispered.

"Oh, no, not again," Norma said.

"I'll be quick tonight, Norma,"
Francine said.

"Only babies talk
to make-believe people,"
said Norma.

Francine pulled the covers
over her head.

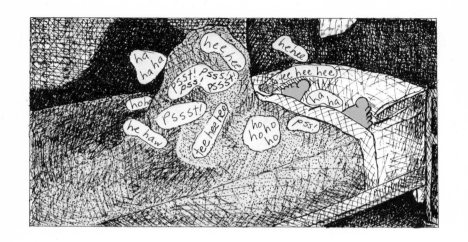

"Bet you won't let me
    talk to him," Norma said.
"He doesn't want to talk to you,"
    Francine shouted
    from under the covers.
    Then all Norma could hear
    were whispers and giggles.

"You're so stupid
I bet you think
he really listens to you,"
Norma said.
She turned over
and went to sleep.

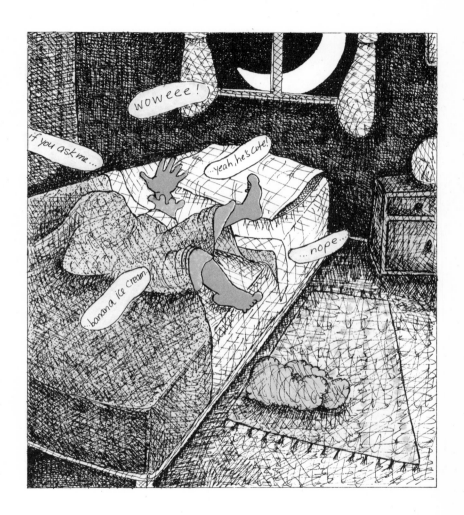

Francine pushed the covers back.
"Good night, Boris," she said.
"I'll speak to you tomorrow."

She put the invisible telephone
back under the bed.

Then she yawned
and went to sleep.

NICKI WEISS makes her debut in the field of children's books with the publication of MENJ!, which she has both written and illustrated.

Graduated from Union College in Schenectady, New York, where she earned extra money baking chocolate chip cookies, Nicki Weiss lived for a time in France. She now lives in New York City, where she was born, and has worked as a textile designer.